The Step Beyond

Robert Buckeye

SPUYTEN DUYVIL
New York City

ISBN 978-1-963908-52-7
cover art: t thilleman

For Jan Galligan

"Speak in whose language? Speak in whose name?"
—T. J. Clark

A door is shut and then another. One by one a long row of them pushed to metal banging metal. Then it is quiet.

The noise of doors shutting. The sound of them crisscrossing up and down the cell block, running ahead of him and then falling back.

These seconds remain fixed in his mind, the cell doors shut behind him; the sound of them echoing again and again in his head; then silence.

Danek had been questioned and searched, put in a paddy wagon, processed in jail. He knew that these things happened, but did not believe that they would happen to him. He noticed his hands folded together on his lap. Everything that had happened had not been normal but seemed as if it was. "Guard, guard," he hears. "I want to call my lawyer." "You can call your lawyer when he calls you," a guard answers.

His thoughts drifted back to why he had been arrested. He could not stop asking himself why it had been him. He worried about Anna. She'd been with him when they had been arrested. He last saw her being taken out of the paddy wagon.

He sank back into the darkness of the cell, drawing himself ever more tightly into himself. He was no longer himself, but a name in a report, a number in a record, a statistic in a filing. They had taken his glasses when he was being processed and without glasses, he could not tell what time it was. He was afraid that if he slept, he would wake and not know where he was.

He had been at a student's apartment after his night class. Coffee had been put on. Sun Ra on a turntable. There was a knock on the door. Two men pushed themselves in. One was a blond with a crew cut who wore a leather vest. The second was a tall, thin man with graying hair who wore a suit under a Trench coat.

They seemed to know we would know why they were here. We asked them to identify themselves, but were told that we would find out soon enough. Danek assumed that they were police. They asked questions, searched the apartment. If he was not under arrest his student said, he was free to leave, but he was stopped before he reached the door.

Danek began to see everything, as if he were not there, but in an apartment across the street looking on. As if he were watching a film and needed to ask someone what was going on. Something he would read in the paper the next day. There was nothing Danek could say that would be held against him, but he knew that whatever he said would be used against him. It was not him, but it was.

Danek had done nothing wrong, but his father would believe that he had. He had been the first in the family to go to college, but the Sixties had come, the Vietnam War had begun, rock and roll and so much more had taken over the land. A time fathers disowned sons and sons left home. His father no longer knew him.

He was released the next day. Photographers waited outside on the street. Microphones were put in his face. What would he say? What would he do? He remembered the contempt on the face of the crewcut officer, what it was like in a paddy wagon, how alone, painfully alone, he felt in the cell. They would not know what it had been like. Unless they were there they would never know.

A Detroit council woman announced a press conference about corruption in the police department the afternoon of his arrest. The next morning *The Detroit Free Press* headline read WSU professor, and 56 others arrested. The press conference of the council woman had been pushed to the back pages of the paper.

The Vice-President of the university suspended him, but the President said at a faculty meeting the next day that the Vice-President had not said what he said. A friend asked him whether he would call the President a liar.

Danek wanted his life back and made every effort to live as he had before. There were weekends with the Johnsons, afternoon coffee with Snyder. Sunday mornings the Times to be read. Anna talked about the

Shakespeare festival in Canada, a weekend at the lake in Oscoda, but they knew it was a way not to talk about what needed to be talked about.

They hired a lawyer to represent them in a false arrest suit against the police. One day they woke up to read in *The Free Press* that they were suing the police for half a million dollars. Their lawyer had not said anything. He left for a *kibbutz* in Israel. We worried that everyone would think we were only in it for money.

Things were no longer the same. They would never be the same again. Black Muslim women walked the streets of Detroit. Coeds posed nude for photographers. One day he read that John Sinclair had been sentenced to ten years in prison for one marijuana cigarette. His student was last heard from in Georgia buying anti-tank guns for the revolution.

Anna wanted nothing to do with it. She had begun work on a graduate degree in Anglo-Saxon and spent her evenings reading *Beowulf*. Late nights Danek listened to Hendrix, "If Six Was Nine."

Danek had found his voice in the classroom, but in front of a class now he no longer knew what to say. He read, but whatever he read did not interest him. He wrote, but did not know what to say or how to say it. A friend asked him to play tennis. He remembered that his parents played pinochle on Saturday nights. It was only a game, but some nights it was more than a game to them.

Days Danek saw himself as the world had seen him on TV. At night he woke thinking he had done something wrong, murdered someone, it might have been a woman and buried her, hoping no one would find her, but when he woke, he could not remember what he had done. It did not stop him from believing it had been him. He had done what he never thought he could do. It went way back, long before he was aware of it.

Danek's contract at the university was not renewed. SUNY Buffalo, which had offered him a position four years before, would only enroll him in a doctoral program now. Trenton State had a position for him, but he never heard from them.

The summer in Detroit was hot. Unemployment was high. Whites increasingly left the city. The police chief asked for more police. Cavanagh would run for President or resign as mayor. Everyone was uneasy. Watts had happened. There would be something in Detroit. They knew there would be.

Danek woke one morning, and it had come. Tanks went down Woodward. Buildings were burning. The Fire Department could not keep up while they were shot at while they worked. The National Guard and police patrolled the streets. The 82nd and 101st airborne were on the other side of town. Helicopters flew overhead. TV did not depend on journalists but reported what they saw out their windows in the studio. A near week of fear, anxiety and insecurity. Then it was over.

We met Willard Maas in the elevator of the guest house of the University of Puerto Rico and shared a Cutty with him in our room. It was the first English we had heard since we arrived that afternoon.

There was nothing Maas did not know. He laughed, but his laugh was less delight than triumph. He was, he said, the best filmmaker in America. Brakhage, Emshwiller, Markopoulos, Mekas. They had learned from him. Hell, he supported them when he had to, gave them his couch, shared his liquor with them.

He nodded for emphasis and gestured with his hands. He was also a poet, but not one of those who practiced *art pour l'art*. He paused to see what we thought. His pink-veined eyes missed nothing.

Writing....His look was brazen. Writing was a descent into parts of yourself you did not know existed. There was no guarantee you would surface and be able to be in the world.

After midnight on our way to a bar off campus, Maas stopped to fondle the genitals of a stray dog.

We learned that Maas had thrown a potted plant through the plate glass window of the student cafeteria and made a long-distance call from a public telephone.

How did he get through, Ellen asked. I haven't been able to get a call through to anyone yet.

Maas refused to attend department meetings, balled up forms and threw them away, stalked out of rooms. Fucking bureaucracy, he would say. Education? What do schools know about it? What the fuck do they know about real education? He had been given a ticket to take him back to New York. The Jean Luc-Godard of Bleeker Street, Ellen said.

Maas did not go back to New York. One day he saw him examining a copy of *Los Hermanos Karamazov* at one of the booksellers outside the gates of the university. A few weeks later he saw him in Old San Juan propositioning a young boy.

Maas had not lied. When he died in 1971, *The New York Times* gave hm an eight-inch obituary. He was a poet, one of the founding members of American independent cinema. His wife, Marina Mencken, starred in Andy Warhol films.

Three Songs From San Juan was the title of Maas's last, unfinished film.

The brown-skinned native in her bikini beckons us southward to the islands. The Madison Avenue dream of El Dorado, lost Atlantis, Prospero's Island. You want Ponce de Leon's fountain of youth? Turn the page.

Bill would have none of it. Screw them all, with a large, syphilitic anger he would say. He twisted his face into a frown, passed a hand across his eyes as if to wave it all away, rubbed his bald head. Good-fucking Christ! Have you ever seen more cretins in your life?

He raised his *Cuba Libre* and swallowed convulsively. Jesus my gut is gone, but I need this. The ass-end of another week. And who is not counting? He looked around at us at our table in this bar in Old San Juan, left eyebrow raised. I may be fucked up, but I mean. I've come to understand whole new levels of the term.

—We know the story, don't we? Bill raised his glass and toasted us. The old Yankee, his blood slowed by too many New England winters, follows the currents in search of a new world, and if he stays long enough, the tropics rot him. You know what happened to Columbus? On his last voyage, so he said, he discovered that the world was not round, but that it was pear-shaped, like a woman's breast, and its nipple was, precisely, the

Amazon basin. Bill shook with hollow laughter. Freud would have made much of that.

Dead-end of a long night. Everyone bleary-eyed, washed-out. Friday night had turned into Saturday morning, and no one would have to teach until Monday. We had had *arroz con pollo, frijoles, flan* at one of the better Puerto Rican restaurants in Old San Juan, had moved over to the Condado for Spanish brandy, espresso and flamenco and then drank *Cuba Libres* in an open-air restaurant across from *La Perla*.

Bill rubbed his eyes, stifled a yawn. Six fucking sleepy-eyed o'clock. As usual, mid-seventies, ten percent chance of rain mid-morning. Paradise. Fucking paradise. Bill squinted down his nose at us. Why the winter of our discontent? He grimaced. His gut was not in good shape with the drinking he had done. Time we moved he said.

The three of us—Bill, Ellen and Danek—had come to teach at the University of Puerto Rico at a point in our lives we needed to step aside, determine what we would do next, but after several months at UPR, realized that we would leave, that the university had been no answer.

A year later we were in Connecticut and Bill told us about *Easy Rider*. We must see it. It was good, although it would have been better if we had seen it stoned. Even then it was depressing. Bill shook his head and rubbed his eyes. The shots that blow Fonda and Hopper away drop the curtain on the dream of Amerca. Talk about punctuation. I can't keep the scene out of my head. Period. End of sentence. End of story.

He looked out the bay window at the rolling hills dark blue in early morning light. The Connecticut countryside was beautiful. He loved living here. It was a pastoral paradise. "As long as one did not look closely," he would add and laugh. Then he turned back to Danek. "We've got to do something."   His deep almond eyes burned, as if he were feverish. "We have to, but fucking Christ, I don't see anything."

Three months later Bill put a plastic bag over his head and tied it off. We were in Indiana then and he was out in the yard when Anna called from the house. It was Ellen on the phone with news about Bill.

He had a bag of cans and bottles to put in the milk cooler by the barn, since we didn't have enough money for the landfill. The corn had been harvested and you could see mice crossing fields to the house. Overhead a hawk glided on air currents. There was a chill in the air, and we did not know whether the furnace would be sufficient for the winter. There would be a frost tonight our neighbor said.

—These shits, these shits who run the government here.

Bernie crossed his legs and looked at us stone-faced. How can they look at themselves in the mirror in the morning? With an overbearing look, he examined us. But we know the answer to that, don't we? His brow furrowed. His anger and contempt. His disappointment.

Greed. Greed, no one had to say, governed all this.

—We write letters to the editor, we protest outside military bases, we speak out, and what good does it do, Bernie asked.

At the end of the Second World War, Bernie Lockwood was stationed in San Juan in air force surveillance to monitor German ships and submarines in the Caribbean. After the war he stayed in San Juan, working for a company that specialized in rescue operations for boats that had capsized and planes that had crashed.

Lockwood was from the Bronx and returned to New York to get a doctorate. He had married a Puerto Rican woman and returned to Puerto Rico to teach at its university in Rio Piedras. He was outspoken for Puerto Rican independence. He began the first film series at the university, showing Italian neo-realist films of the fifties and sixties that had not been seen in Puerto Rico before

Several of his students followed Lockwood to New York to study for doctorates and returned to the island to teach. Over time they began to assume the role of fighting not only for the education of Puerto Ricans, but also their independence. Lockwood had become a legend in the department but gave way to the new generation.

Danek met Bernie Lockwood the year he taught at UPR and would return to see him and other friends. One summer Alicia, Bernie's wife, called to tell him Bernie would not live much longer. He flew to San Juan to see Bernie one last time. Not much was said because there was nothing any longer to be said. We'd known each other a long time, things were not good now, but when had they ever been good.

The German walked across the street stopping for a moment to look back to the *avenida* at the end of the *calle* before he walked to a *playa*. His father, a University of Chicago graduate, had come to Puerto Rico before the First World War to teach school in the mountains of Puerto Rico near Yauco and he had followed his father until he retired and had come down to San Juan.

He was man of habit. He believed in order. Every morning, he came down to the *playa* at dawn. He lunched at one of the few restaurants on O'Leary to serve Puerto Rican food and every day ate the same meal. Rice and beans, chicken, a beer, followed by espresso. At four he played chess there on the terrace with a *viejo independista*. It was a struggle between the man of reason and the man of passion, the icy north and hot-blooded tropics, the old world and the new. At nine each evening he drank brandy until his head slumped to the table.

Jane Miller. He should meet her, Bernie said. He would not have said anything if he didn't think we would get along. He did not have to say why. Danek had a sense she was not like Bernie Lockwood. Bernie was drawn to her because she was what he would be, if he was not who he was.

We were to meet at a commemoration of a new art building on the UPR campus. She was late. Before she left her apartment she had gone for a run and been attacked by a dog. There was blood on her leg. She should get it treated, but she told me not to worry.

She was not sure that she would come but did not want to disappoint Bernie. Bernie assured her she would like him. She glanced at Danek to make sure that he was the one she should meet but saw someone over his shoulder. She had to see him. If she did not....

He was leaving for a conference on Nevis and there would not be time to talk to him about class size. She looked for him to see if he was still there. She turned back to Danek and said she would see him later. He did not see her before he left. A short, dark-haired woman in her thirties with a ready smile and a laugh no one could miss.

It was, Danek learned later, characteristic. Miller was mercurial. What she did now was not what she did next. What came later had to be done now. She began to do something else before she had finished what she had been doing.

We met at a bar off campus in Rio Piedras on a Sunday afternoon in May. Bernie was right. It was as if we met the one in our life we needed to know. The talk of those who need to talk and cannot stop. So much depends on it. One could say everything does.

Miller was working-class. She knew from the beginning that she would not be a waitress, a secretary, a clerk. The curse of the working class was that we would never be good enough. She looked at the glass in her hand. It was not until she went to college that she knew what she would do.

She glanced at Danek, as if she could see what she needed to say. It was a story she felt he knew. The reading she did. What she thought, heard, saw. Those she met. Her world was no longer that of a farm girl living down a deserted road in the country.

Teaching let her be herself in a way she could not be in any other work. It was uncanny. She saw in her students her own life, as if she was there to teach them what she had not been taught. When she stood in front of a class....

She stopped and thought for a moment about what she had been saying. She laughed. She pointed to the bartender. She would have another gin-and-tonic. We knew, did we not, that we did not teach, as if we were Robinson Crusoe on a deserted island. Would he have another?

We work in an educational system that reflects national interests and priorities. Isn't that how it goes? She glanced at the gin-and-tonic on the table in front of her. Class, gender and race were the elephants in the room that were not talked about. We know that. We know it all too well.

We looked at one another, looked away. This moment was rare, even if it would not last. That we had this talk was a sign that it was possible, even necessary, to claim our lives for ourselves. What the rich claim for themselves without having to acknowledge that it had been given them at the beginning.

Several years later Bernie wrote to tell him that Miller had been let go. The administration was glad to see her go. She was not conservative enough. She took the side of students when it was not political to take their side. Damned for being herself and damned for not being one of them

Jane Miller stays with him. It had only been one afternoon in a bar in Rio Piedras. One afternoon in a life. There are moments, however, moments complete in themselves, that stay with us. The longer he thought about Jane Miller, the more he understood that he, too, would be let go.

It came sooner than he thought it would come. After UPR, he was given a one-year contract at UConn. A fill-in at the last moment. The next year he was living in a deserted farmhouse down a dirt road in Indiana. He would walk its fields asking himself what was next. He remembered what it had been like in a cell in the Detroit jail when he had been arrested.

A foreshadowing that went back to the day in school he heard *hunky, bohunk, you* for the first time, knowing it was him they meant. That went back to bitter cold days on his way to school where he would tuck his chin down on his pea coat to keep warm. Mother would tell him to hold his head up. Be proud you're a Danek. She would not accept what she refused to acknowledge.

Bernie wrote and said Jane Miller was in Maine. He did not know why or what she was doing. A few years later she was dead. It's not enough, I hear her say. Never enough. And she laughed, delighted by her laugh. She never thought that enough would be too much.

In 1970 he went to a rally at UConn to support Bobby Seale, who was being held for murder in New Haven. Jean Genet, who had come into the country illegally, spoke. A Black Panther spoke. It might have been Hilliard. The other Panther officers were in jail. Half an hour into the rally someone said something to one of those on the platform. He got up and said something to Hilliard who was at the podium. There has been a bomb threat, Hilliard said. The police advised us to move to another building. He paused, looked down at a virtually white middle-class audience. Danek was sitting too far back to see the look on Hilliard's face. As far as I am concerned, he said, your white asses would do more for the revolution dead than alive. We did not move and in a moment, Hilliard continued his talk.

It had been a spring day in Indiana. A brilliant, clear blue spring day. A few slashes of crowd across the sky. Anna came out of the kitchen. Some students had been shot at Kent State.

Overhead a hawk floated on the currents of air. A chipmunk darted out of the barn. Across the road our neighbor waved from his tractor. Danek waved back and looked at Anna. Her jaw was stern, her lips held tightly together. There was anger in her gaze, uncertainty, a touch of anxiety.

We did not know it then, but it was the end of something. The assassinations of King, Kennedy, his brother, Danek's arrest, riots in Detroit, Los Angeles and so many other places, the Vietnam War had sent us to this farmhouse in Indiana.

We had become short with one another, cynical with friends, dismissive, curt with others. We had to step back, step away. When a friend offered his grandparents' farmhouse in Indiana rent-free—it had not been lived in for a quarter century—we had no choice. Danek had not been offered a teaching job. The library at UConn where Anna worked was cutting back.

In Indiana, we could not escape America, no matter

how much we thought we would. Paul Harvey was on the radio mornings before stock prices. The farmer across the road said nothing, but we knew he did not care for anyone who did not work. We would never convince him that the money we had was money earned. In town, people stared, their lips tight. Danek had a beard. Anna went bra-less.

Our water was sulphuric. It tasted like rotten eggs. When the pump failed, we used the outhouse, gathered snow to boil water. The coal furnace gave up the ghost, but we were able to get a cheap electric furnace at Sears by applying for their credit card. It heated only the dining room. We did not take baths because the water cooled before the tub was filled. Friends said they wished they could do what we did.

By spring we learned we could live there, but we did not know what that meant. The Indiana county we lived in was staunch, right-wind Republican. The Klu Klux Klan was active in Kokomo. We were not farmers. If there was a separate peace, we did not see it.

Some mornings from the spare room on the second floor Danek had made his study, he would see a train, smoke trailing behind it, make its way slowly through corn fields. A locomotive one saw in Hollywood Westerns, but smaller. At a distance, the size of a model train in one's basement.

He did not know where the train went or what it carried. The longer he saw it the more he knew we would leave. It was going somewhere. We were not, but could not accept what our lives had become, although some days we asked ourselves why. Every day the train chugchugged through corn. We waited for it.

Friends came, and it was like old times, except it was not old times. They had continued with their lives, and we had not. We had a past we shared. We were a future they would not risk. They had a present, but we did not know what to do with ours. We talked about what was happening in the country but skirted around what was happening to us in the farmhouse. They could not understand what we were doing. We no longer did.

Kent State sent us back into the world, not because we had to do something but because we despaired of doing anything. We could no longer live alone with it in Indiana with Paul Harvey on the radio and the contempt on the faces of those on the streets of the town.

We came back east. We went to work. Did what we

did not feel bad about. The world we lived in before would be the distraction we needed. It would permit us to escape ourselves. We knew we led privileged lives and did nothing about our privilege except to let it shelter us, even though we tried to fool ourselves into believing otherwise. We wrote letters to the editor, gave money to the right candidates, went to the natural foods co-op, did not buy stocks.

We asked ourselves why we had come back. We screamed at one another, but it did not conceal our anguish. Our increasing silence said what was said. We no longer looked at one another.

If we were to get our lives back, whatever those lives might be, we could no longer go back to the beginning. If we were to begin again, it would have to be somewhere else, something else and—we could not say it to one another—with someone else.

Anna had been visiting her family in Cleveland at Christmas. They would ask why he was not with her, but she would say he had work to do. When he picked her up at the airport, we stopped to get something to eat at Burger Chef before going home. While we waited for our food, we looked at one another. Anna's pale blue, cobalt eyes on him. Those eyes that confronted him the first time he saw her. And you her glance always asked. You?

Did she say it or did he? It made no difference. It was over.

Elena, Leni. One day she came to the library and asked Danek about a book. He had seen in her town. She was attractive, with short, curly black hair, cobalt blue eyes, dimpled cheeks, a distant smile on her face, delicately shaped breasts. Her laughter bubbled up at odd moments, husky and full.

The next time they said hello. They talked. She asked him about a book. He spoke of Dostoyevsky. She of Tolstoy. There was Flaubert. If not Virginia Woolf. If she were to look at. Not if he had not read.

They had coffee in cafes. They talked more. They saw *Annie Hall* more than once, laughed together as with no one else. Then. A quick embrace. A wet kiss full or promise. She smiled.

Before they understood what their talk said. She put her hand on his. Before it could be answered. She cannot fuck anyone. She laughed. At moments though she cannot resist when the moment presents itself. There must be. For a moment she smiled as if she remembered something. There must be.

What could not be silenced sat alongside them for months, demanding it be answered, real as it had not been at the beginning. They would not have been lovers had they not talked for months. Their talk was real, as most talk is not. It had an urgency that did not rush past itself. As if what was said could be said only in the time of its time. She knew exactly who he was. He was the man who said no but would not say no to her.

He never thought anything would happen. He may have inadvertently touched her breast or touched her hand to emphasize something he said. He thought of what it would be like, but that did not mean....

They talked. All they had done was talk.

She'd come to his apartment. It had not been the first time. They talked and drank wine. He touched her hand to make a point. She ran a finger across her lip before she said. She looked at the clock. It was late. She rolled her eyes. He laughed. The bottle was empty. He opened another. He does not remember who first leaned across the couch. They kissed. It seemed no more than a moment.

He had come out of the bathroom after they had made love and not knowing what he would say said that this was not playing, he wanted them to risk something, that there was too much compromise in life, too much sacrifice of desire to comfort, and he was sick of it. Leni sat on a chair with one leg lifted, her foot on the seat, her chin resting on a knee, and looked at him in a way he did not understand.

The nights he looked at her after they made love, a slight smile on her face, the tip of her tongue against her upper lip, breath a whisper. Sound of Hovaness on a late-night Albany FM station. Her skin luminous in moonlight.

If there is one man for Elana Danek learned, there must be one another. There must be at least two. If one leaves, there is always one left. She would never be left alone again, as she had been in college. She would not slit her wrists again, as she had then.

There was her husband, and if he were no longer her husband, there would be another husband. There would always be a husband. Elana could not be other than who she was. Danek could not be other than who he was.

Elana had never answered him the night he came out of the bathroom after they had made love, but they had risked something only for her to step back before it went further. She left for Boston with her husband before the end of the year.

Fitzgerald was Judith Fitzgerald, a poet at Deer Track in 1980, a makeshift writers' conference at a recreational area in rolling hills outside South Bend. Everyone slept on the ground in bed rolls or in tents.

Deer Track was the nowhere they had to be. The nowhere their writing needed to know itself. What those men Danek saw huddled over desks in large, urban public libraries, bundled slips of paper wrapped in rubber bands on desks in front of them, knew. An urgency they could not let go. "The community," Avital Ronell writes, "of those without community."

There was a black postal worker from Chicago at Deer Track. He did not know punctuation, grammar or spelling, but his description of a fence post with ice on it in winter or sunrise over Lake Michigan was real. What he wrote could not be taught. It was itself in itself.

Deer Track marked the trail. A constellation that formed around them. They would write to one another. On his way back to Vermont from seeing his brother in Ypsilanti, he would stop and see Fitzgerald in Toronto.

Fitzgerald began a dissertation on Charles Olson and if we can say that her poetry shows she has read Olson well, it explains why she did not finish her thesis on

Olson. References to Olson affix themselves like post-it notes to her poems in a dialogue she maintains with him.

For a poet whose subject is often may be love, the question of whether she can love a man, "who knows nothing of Olson," is, if not significant, at least not idle.

The conversation she carries on with Olson slowly but surely marks a turning away from him, even if she cannot escape him. She sees herself to be "a displaced Salesian [who] wanders Dogtown."

There were reasons why Fitzgerald would be drawn to Olson. For both the absent father is crucial. Fitzgerald's father left after she was born. She never knew who he was and finds stepfathers in a succession of beds, which are never one-night stands, but re-enactments of some primal scene, whether for absolution or transcendence, she never knows.

If the absence of the father, however it has come about, is rejection, their search for fathers also leads them to reject fathers: the state, academy, literature.

"Where I come from," Fitzgerald says. She did not know her father, her mother worked as a prostitute and went mad. In school, her test scores were dismissed.

A genealogy that determined what she saw, how she listened. The mistake she would embrace. A Cabbagetown ethos. She would be, "no suburban and manicured intelligence." A poetry at the end of the road.

One night in Toronto he remembers Fitzgerald picked up her bag and rummaged through it in search of something. For a moment she looked across the room as if she recognized somebody but was not certain who it was. Her face was devastated, as if she had seen him before, would always see him, and she would not know who it was.

In his cabin in the woods outside Temple, Maine, Ted Enslin had no electricity, split wood for heat, walked two hundred yards to a stream to get water. For several years they wrote to one another every month, sometimes every week. The post office for Enslin was a five-mile walk. He talked to himself, Mitch Goodman told him, sang. If he was to write, he told Mitch, he must not only do with less, but also follow the lesson of less.

In a clearing in the woods on their way to the Enslin cabin, they saw a house and barn, a garden nearby with a man working in it. There were chickens and goats in the yard, and a cow in a nearby field.

When the man saw us, he waved and came over to us. He had been an aerospace engineer for Boeing but at some point, became anxious. If there was another war. He spoke of world-wide destruction, toxic radiation, poisoned water, people and plants dying

He remembered that he had grown up with Civil Defense drills and air-raid shelters and nightmares of the big bomb. The promise of the end of the world was the only one they had been given.

If there was a nuclear war.... For a moment he wiped his forehead with a rag. He would survive. He nodded.

Yes, he would. He smiled. He'd been here fifteen years. It had not been easy at first but what was. He was free now as he had not been at Boeing.

At some point his wife could no longer take it and left with their two sons. He did not mind living by himself, but at some point he knew he needed someone. He went to dances in town, joined clubs, went to church, answered ads.

He met women, but it did not work out with those he met. A smile crossed his face. They found him different. He laughed. Strange. For a moment he looked at the house. His eyes deep pools. For a moment he seemed to think about what he said. But one day....He looked at us for a moment.

One day a woman will walk down this path as you have done, see my house and garden and say to herself, this is where I want to be.

Danek would think of Enslin in his cabin, splitting wood, getting water, talking to himself and to the world, singing a lyric from Nadia Boulanger he learned, and writing, always writing. He remembered a line from one of Enslin's poems that Enslin read when he was at Deer Track. "It is always the middle ground, the compromise that destroys." Enslin could write beyond himself only if he remained inside himself. A poetic line that emphasized words—but, not, or, no—for emphasis, as in a musical composition. (Before he became a poet, Enslin studied musical composition with Boulanger.)

Near the Metcalf home on Quarry Road, there is an abandoned quarry not visible from the road, and the climb an effort, but it was one of the sites one had to see when he visited the Metcalfs. As one approached the quarry, one began to see the abandoned machines of the industry, thin gauge tracks, conveyor belts, pulleys, channeling machines and drills until, all of a sudden, one came to the pit, the drop to the water, precipitous and deep. It was more primeval than the forest, and if it was difficult to imagine that at one time the mountainside was filled with men and the sounds of work, it was also not possible to be quieted. Here on a mountain the woods had long reclaimed the mark of man.

During a weekend, we would drive to Chester to get more beer and wine and pick up a Sunday paper, and on these trips, Paul Metcalf would comment about who lived in this or that house, how they made a living, how long they had lived on Quarry Road. He would also point out the fresh gashes in the forest, the land that a Princeton academic or a New York lawyer had acquired for a summer home.

Gradually, summer after summer, the landscape of Quarry Road changed. Those who had been there from the beginning eked out even less than they had before, and their homes became run-down, often deserted. Those who discovered this undeveloped corner of the Berkshires more recently came in greater numbers to build their homes, although they never got the road repaired.

It has been one of Metcalf's achievements as a writer to locate those quarries that time and history have lost, and to keep track of those progress had displaced. Down those by-ways that county road commissioners don't feel they have to repair, if they even remember them, and by houses that look, to the careless eye, deserted, so that to see someone around them is to think them an intruder.

In the deserted house we stumble on in the woods, we may take a cup from the sink, left how many months or even years before, or examine a framed photograph that has fallen to the floor, and—inexplicably, it is an uncanny sense—not that someone is there, but we feel we are not alone. It is the space Metcalf's writing occupies.

Renee, the bartender, comes from the Eastern Townships. You want another bourbon, she asks Danek. Herve, who was reading Hannah Arendt's *Eichmann in Jerusalem* when Danek sat down next to him, told him he is here Friday and Saturday nights. He is French, from Brittany, works as a software programmer and was in Bangkok last year. He waves a hand around the bar. This year it is Montreal. He does not know where he will be next year.

George is an engineer who worked on the Prince Edward Island bridge. He comes from a small town in Ottawa but won't go back. He is a big man, with a burnt, chiseled face like granite, rust-brown hair that spills onto his forehead, thick, calloused hands. My mother's mother lived down the street, he says. You never escaped. He drinks beer.

My grade schoolteacher not only taught the parents of her students but their parents as well. I knew how he would turn out she would say about a drunk in town, a man who had left his wife, one whose business had failed.

Danek tells them he is from Vermont. You need to get to Montreal, George says. I know what small towns

47

are like. Seven, eight times a year Danek says. For a moment he runs a hand over his balding head. He laughs.

I had to leave, Renee says. I saw what my mother's life was like. She puts her elbows on the bar and leans forward. I was not going to spend my life in a small town. Wryly she miles. I sang in a church choir when I first got to Montreal.

At least you stay in one place for a year, George says to Herve. I may be in Vancouver for a month, move over to Calgary, fly to Labrador while I'm still working in Calgary. He finishes his beer and gestures to Renee for another. The hotel I'm in looks like the one I was in yesterday. I can tell you where the bed will be, what the bedspread looks like.

Some days I ask myself what city I'm in or what day of the week it is. On a project i may work weekends and evenings. He wipes his forehead with a handkerchief. I should be packed and shipped. For a moment he looks at something on the other side of the bar. Some days I feel I have.

I want to travel, Renee says. A guy took me to Plattsburgh one day. I might as well have been in the

Eastern Townships. She goes over to a table to fill a drink order. When she returns, she raises her eyebrows in a question to Danek. Another bourbon? It's difficult for a young, single woman to travel.

We're not from Montreal, George says. We don't know anyone. We go to a bar, watch *Les Canadiennses* on tv, say something to the guy next to us. We go back to the hotel and watch more television, finish a beer.

The evening is still young. We go out again. This time we may look for a woman. He runs a hand through his hair. Everyone in a bar is passing through. Tomorrow we won't be here. Someone else will be in your place. Renee will be talking to him. If she's still here.

At SUNY Buffalo, Ken Warren studied under Creeley and John Clarke before he became a librarian in Texas first, then in Lakewood, a suburb of Cleveland, "a deep, dark city on a great lake," he wrote in a letter to Danek, "in which I can prowl the night and do an occasional radio show on the college fm...I am drawn to the unfamiliar city more than anything else, hitting its bars, talking and listening."

In an unpublished work titled, *The Rap on the Door*, he refers to that moment that determines what we do if we but answer it. It is definitive but we may not know that it is until we understand where it has led us. The weight that cannot be borne until it is.

Warren was led to what was not read or thought as much as that that was. The Dominican Sisters led him to God, Catholicism, William Blake; Pound to Olson to Ferrini; Freud to Jung to James Hillman and much else, alchemy, astrology; Shao Lin and Tai Chi to leafy vegetables to livers, kidneys; New York to Buffalo to Waco to Lakewood and back to Buffalo again, "following the poet with no place special to go, save the sea, the road." "Nowhere to Run" was the title of one of his poems.

He was, he said, a sandlot scholar, who took his bat and ball out of the classroom and into the streets where we live. In his day job as a librarian, he understood that a public library was not only a warehouse but also an alternative. "Community's most dignified haven for labor unfit for the rigors; of the business world," he writes, "the preferred workplace, that is, for the eccentric brother, the infirm spouse, a shy daughter." At night in Cleveland, he played punk music on late night radio, identifying himself as Bagworm.

Danek had come to New York to hear Meridel Le Sueur speak at a feminist gathering in the West Village. He saw Joe Napora who introduced him to Warren. Three men among more than a hundred women. Our presence was an offence, but we understood that the only way to keep ourselves in a society that takes away who we are, that values what cannot be valued, that may enslave us in its very act of setting us free was to stand where we stood.

Warren was always there. He showed us ways. He knew that we could go farther than we thought we could and walked alongside us as we did. The last time we talked on the phone, he said we would not leave a

mark, but it was crucial that we did not, Olson, always
Olson, in the background:

> In the land of plenty, have
> Nothing to do with it
>
>   take the way of
>
> the lowest,
> including
> your legs, go
> contrary, go
>
> sing

House Organ, the journal Warren edited for more than
twenty years, his signature Kilroy, published writing
that fit uncomfortably elsewhere, if it fit at all, but had
a place with him. It also gave readers an opportunity
to be schooled by Warren. In each issue, he addressed
Olson, Ferrini, Olson, again and again Olson, but also
Eshleman, Codrescu.

Warren is no longer there, but one night, late, very
late, he will hear a voice on some talk radio show, or a

punk music station announce himself as Bagworm and know who it is.

Danek had just seen Peter Watkins' film on Strindberg, more than three hours long, on wooden risers in a room at the back of a cafe on St. Laurent. A disturbing film, particularly of Strindberg's last days in Paris, alone, endlessly doing scientific experiments. He had been driven to do more. It had not been enough, but he would not stop until it was enough.

Most of those in the small audience were Swedish, who, it seemed to Danek did not know film but wanted to see images of Sweden and hear their native language, as they did not hear it in Montreal. After the intermission, most of them were gone. After the film was over, he stayed, wanting to let Watkins' provocative and unsettling film sit with him a moment longer before he left.

When he turned to leave, he saw a woman sitting in the back row, moved by Watkins' film as he had been. He wanted to say something to her but left without saying anything. It would have been wrong. What they thought could not be shared.

On Sherbrooke Street on his way back to the hotel, he heard music on a side street. It was not rock or jazz, not punk, but music that came from somewhere else, out of a dim past he thought he recognized. Music meant to excite as much as it threatened. Anything was possible, it said. Nothing was held back.

There was no light on any of the buildings in the block. There were no signs. The sound of the music from one of the buildings was insistent, demanding, relentless. Do you want it the sax cried. Do you want it? It brought back the night that gave us back ourselves as much as it aroused the fear of what the night brings. Danek found himself in a cafe with a band at one end, consisting of a sax, violin, accordion and drums, and a bar on the other side.

Come, the voice of the singer said. Come. His glance on a woman at a table near him. She was close to middle-age in a pale blue, floor-length dress. She got up, took a step towards him, then a second step before she began to move, slowly at first, shifting her hips back and forth.

The violinist moved close to her and brought his violin near her face. Slowly they moved, the violin leading and the woman following. As if the woman was as much the music as the violin and each, in turn, took the lead from the other. Her arms described arcs, arabesques, geometries. They explored the space in front of her, reaching out, tentatively, pausing, turning, finding direction, an aimlessness waiting to find itself, search without goal. As if her hands needed to touch the space in front of her, hold it, know it as she knows a lover's body.

The singer clasped his hands together, the beat picked up, his voice rising. The violinist bowed furiously. The sax chased after itself. The accordion kept the beat. The woman stamped her feet, threw her arms about wildly, claimed the world as hers, a dervish possessed. Less a dance than a ritual act.

You must enter the music before it can enter you, it said. Before it can send you down a path, cut a trail for you. Written on your skin, shaping memory and dream. The bass carrying the beat. The sax chasing itself. Drums crashing. Written on your skin, shaping memory and dream.

It was the Cafe Sarajevo and brought with it fear of the mysterious East, of what we did not know, of what we want as much as we fear. The films of Kusturica and the horror of Sarajevo in the news every day. A history always there but never forgotten. Those who came were there every weekend. What was lost, what had been buried, was brought back for them in Cafe Sarajevo.

When Danek was in Montreal he would be at Cafe Sarajevo until it shut down. He would see those who would not miss a night at Cafe Sarajevo. They understood why they were there and in one way or another would acknowledge one another. When the drummer saw him, he knew who Danek was. A waitress would bring over his bourbon without him having to order it.

Then it shut down. The owner had come to Montreal from Sarajevo and bought the run-down building on Clark Street. His apartment was above the Cafe. A third apartment was reserved for ex-pats. No one knew why he closed the cafe or where he went. It was as if Cafe Sarajevo was of its time until its time ran out. A today that had a yesterday that determined what it would be was no longer there. Leave, he must have thought. It was time.

ROBERT BUCKEYE is author of five works of fiction about Puerto Rico (*Pressure Drop*), the Kent State shootings (*Still Lives*), Edvard Munch (*The Munch Case*), Bratislava (*Fade*), and the novel *Not Her Nor Him*, as well as a study of the English novelist, Ann Quin (*Re: Quin*). In 2015, Spuyten Duyvil published a collection of his criticism, *Living In*. *The Grocery Store on Lasaretska Street* is a continuation of *Nightfall*, also published by Spuyten duyvil. He divides his time between Vermont and Bratislava.